For Hilary Delamere
HC

For my nieces and nephews: Hannah, Adam, Sophie, Thomas, and James
GS

Candlewick Studio, an imprint of Candlewick Press   99 Dover Street   Somerville, Massachusetts 02144   www.candlewickstudio.com
Printed in Humen, Dongguan, China   21 22 23 24 25 26 APS 10 9 8 7 6 5 4 3 2 1

SAVING THE
BUTTERFLY

HELEN COOPER   ILLUSTRATED BY GILL SMITH

CANDLEWICK STUDIO
an imprint of Candlewick Press

There were two of them left in the boat.

A little one and a bigger one.

Brother and sister, lost in the dark sea.

They could have died.

The bigger one thought they wouldn't survive.

But they did.

They were rescued.

The little one never remembered much about it:

kind hands carrying them to land;

sleeping while the bigger one did the speaking.

Somehow she sorted everything out.

Someone helped.

Someone else found them shelter.

A broken house.

The bigger one said they were lucky.

They could have lost even more.

Yet they had nothing.

Or almost nothing.

Nothing left from before,

except each other.

The little one didn't think about that for long.

But the bigger one did.

She couldn't help it.

Months went on.
The little one made friends,
grew strong,
and laughed.
He hardly ever thought about the time before.

But the bigger one couldn't forget.
She felt she shouldn't forget.
Over her mind a shadow fell,
and a squeezing in her chest
sometimes made it hard to breathe.

She hid away in their broken house,
feeling safer there,
in the real dark,
hiding from the dark
in her mind.
After a while she hardly ever
came out.

The little one didn't know how to help.
He wanted to bring her the outside
(the beautiful outside),
so he caught a butterfly
and carried it back to their
broken house . . .

She told him to set it free.

The little one cried.

And the butterfly wouldn't leave.

It battered and smashed its pretty wings against the walls.

Panicking!

"Give it space," said the bigger one.

"Give it time."

After a while the butterfly tired
and settled.
Tiptoeing, the little one almost trapped it.

But the butterfly turned on him:
flicking its wings, making an angry whispering sound,
and now its rainbow markings seemed like watching eyes.

Frightened, the little one hurried outside.
"Come away," he begged his sister.
He didn't want to leave her there.

"I can't," said the bigger one. "Not yet."

Rain pattered.

The bigger one waited.

Shadows and worries clutched her again.

Usually she breathed deep and counted to ten.

That day, instead, she counted the colors

on the butterfly's wing,

one color for each breath.

The butterfly was quiet.

She opened the door . . .

"Shoo!" she said. The butterfly fluttered twice

around the room. Then landed on her hand.

It wouldn't move.

She knew what she ought to do.

She wasn't ready to go,

but would she ever be?

Breathing deep,

counting the colors on the butterfly's wing,

she stepped into the rain.

Still that pesky butterfly clung to her hand.

Until she took a huge breath

and blew.

Then the butterfly flew.

Up into a shaft of sun and the arch of a sudden rainbow.

The butterfly didn't look back.

She wished she didn't have to look back,

but memories and shadows called

from the dark safety in the broken house.

Just then the little one saw her.

And he called her too.

She didn't know if she could reach him as the rainbow faded.